The Dad Book

WRITTEN AND ILLUSTRATED BY

For dads everywhere. Keep up the good work. Even though it may seem rough at times, you are needed, loved, and important.

PANCHO RUCKER

"Finally, I can get some time to myself to sit back and enjoy doing nothing." Daddy said as he sat down from a long day of work.

He couldn't wait to embrace the couch, get on his laptop, and enjoy being left alone. "I got my drink, my special Buie Snacks, and my laptop. Let's start the ---"

"What the fuck?!" Daddy whispers to himself.

The big and loud voice startled him. It was unexpected and caught him off guard. It couldn't be anybody but his baby girl Belle. He could spot her voice anywhere and I mean ANY-WHERE. Like if there was a pack of wild banshees arguing on microphones and Belle yelled out something he could legibly hear EVERY SYLLABLE that she said with NO issue.

"Yes my beautiful Baby Belle?" he said.
"DADDY, I WANT MY TAAAAABLET! I can't find it!" Belle said.
She was distraught and needed assistance.
"Well baby, where did you put it last?" Daddy asked.
"Th-th-th-the bed!" Belle replied while trying to calm herself
down.

Daddy looked on the bed and seen her lime green tablet on the bed next to Mommy.

Mommy was looking like a snack while reading her book with a silk bonnet on her head. Daddy wanted nothing more but to mess her hair, which she just got done, right on up but he had to focus on the task… Baby Belle needed a hero.

"Baby Belle," Daddy said, "The tablet is in the bed next to Mommy did you know that?"

"Yes sir." Belle looked up with the sweetest voice.

"Well, you know that you can get it yourself, right?" Daddy asked.

"Yes sir," said Baby Belle.

"So why haven't you yet?" He asked.

"Because I want Mommy to get it." Baby Belle replied.
"Mannnnnn if you don't GETCHO lil ummm…" Daddy cuts himself
off before he finishes.

Daddy gets back to the couch to start the festivities of doing nothing. "Finally, I can get back to the task at hand. ABSOLUTELY NOTHING!" He said. "With that being said time to eat this 'special' red velvet Buie Snack and get hi---"

"Got damn it what now?" he asked himself.
Another loud thump came from another room but this time it came from Junior's room. "Th'Fuck is he doing in there? Riverdancing?"

Daddy goes to investigate the disturbance.

The moment he opens the door, the stench of puberty, farts, and gamer sweat fills his nostrils. Among the array of unsavory fragrances, was Junior playing a video game. For some reason though, he stood directly in front of the tv. Like "I could taste the serial number if I yawned" close.

"What the hell are you doing son?" Daddy asked.

"I'm playing Deathkill Online and some kid just planted flowers in my murder garden so now I have to assassinate his grandmother and future past him." Junior emphatically said.

"Oooooooooh ok. I have no idea what the hell you just told me. But hey, I have a couple of questions for you son." Daddy stated.

"Sure dad" the little replied.

"Ok. Now hear me out here son, these questions are from a place of love." He said, trying to find the words to tell his son. "First. Why are you so close to the TV? Didn't your mom just buy you a pair of glasses? I guess you wanted the game to be in 3D huh? Are you trying to dry hump the TV? I don't think the TV is comfortable with you being that close."

Junior looked puzzled as dad went on with his Kanye-like rant of questions he continued to ask. "Next son, why does it smell like fuck me tender in here? Bro, it smells like you hate yourself. You spend all day playing on that damn 'Entendoo' that you forgot that at least once a day, water and soap needs to touch that ass?" Dad went on. "Matter of fact, turn that damn game off and go make love to the shower then take your ass to bed. You've got school tomorrow."

"Yes sir." Junior replies. He turns off the game and prepares for his shower.

In the other room, a sweet aroma of perfume grabs Daddy's attention. Immediately, he follows his nose to the scene of the crime to find Mommy. She was getting her a soda out of the fridge.

"Oww boy that hurt." She laughs.
"What I tell you about leaving all that ass out? You were
begging for it." Daddy replied, "Now come here."

"Don't start something you can't finish, now" she says "You know we got a warden that doesn't like physical contact with the opposite sex."

"Man, fuck them kids," Daddy said as he kisses her on the neck. "Girl I got something for you. Now lemme do what I gotta---"As he tried to finish his sentence he feels a tug on his shorts.

"Daddy, it's time for mommy to come to bed now, I'm sleepy," Belle says.
"Can you give mommy a second sweetheart? Daddy needs to talk to her." Daddy asked Belle. However, his efforts fell flat faster than a deflated tire.

"NO! Mommy needs to come to bed!" Belle says.
"I told you. Duty calls." Mommy says. "But I tell you what, wake me up if I fall asleep with her."
"Ok, baby." Daddy replied, but he knew that meant that he would not have any success tonight.

Now back on the couch, daddy looked around and saw that everyone was asleep. He was happy that he finally got to do what he wanted to do....

RELAX!